DATE DUE

Time Goes By

A Day in a
City

Nicholas Harris

Ⓜ Millbrook Press / Minneapolis

First American edition published in 2009 by Lerner Publishing Group, Inc.

Copyright © 2004 by Orpheus Books Ltd.

Millbrook Press
A division of Lerner Publishing Group, Inc.
241 First Avenue North
Minneapolis, MN 55401 USA

Website address: www.lernerbooks.com

Library of Congress Cataloging-in-Publication Data

Harris, Nicholas.
    A day in a city / by Nicholas Harris. — 1st American ed.
      p.   cm. — (Time goes by)
    Summary: text and bird's-eye-view illustrations portray a busy day in a city, including
activities at a school, an apartment building, a theater, and a museum. Includes related activities.
Includes index
      ISBN 978–1–58013–552–8 (lib. bdg. : alk. paper)
    1. City and town life—Fiction. I. Title
PZ7.H24339 2009
[E]—dc22   2008000627

Manufactured in the United States of America
1 2 3 4 5 6 — BP — 14 13 12 11 10 09

Table of Contents

THIS IS THE STORY of

a day in a city. All the pictures have exactly the same view. But each one shows a different time of day. Lots of things happen during this day. Can you spot them all?

Some pictures have parts of the walls taken away. This helps you see inside the buildings.

As you read, look for people who appear throughout the day. For example, keep your eye on one of the office workers. He never leaves his desk. And watch for the burglar wearing a mask. His day doesn't turn out the way he planned. Think about what stories these people might tell about living in a city.

You can follow all the action in the city from morning to night. The clock on each right-hand page tells you what time it is.

The city is filled with action all day long. Shoppers, students, and workers come and go. The cats and dogs in the neighborhood have a busy day too. There's always something new to find!

Can you
find . . .

a sleepwalker?

Early in the morning, most people are asleep. But a few are out and about already. A dog enjoys chasing two early-morning runners. The street cleaners are at work. One poor man has been working in his office all night. Another night worker, a burglar, is just returning home. He had a busy night robbing people's houses.

6:00 A.M.

Early morning

Rush hour

The workday begins

Midmorning

Lunchtime

A rainy afternoon

Evening

Nighttime

Can you find . . .

a newsstand?

the burglar?

Traffic fills the streets. Everyone is on the move. Men and women travel to work. Children make their way to school. Two cars have an accident on the corner. The crash blocks traffic. Meanwhile, people selling goods set up tables at the market. Workers clean up the theater and the museum. A cleaner at the museum does not notice some strange things happening behind her back.

8:00 A.M.

Early morning

Rush hour

The workday begins

Midmorning

Lunchtime

A rainy afternoon

Evening

Nighttime

a break-dancer?

an office worker?

a motor scooter?

The working day has begun. At school, the first class is starting. The shops are open for business. A rehearsal begins at the theater. The office workers are at their desks. Above them, two sculptors are forming something from gray clay. What will it be? Outside, the traffic has snarled to a halt. A truck is towing one of the crashed cars. Some roadwork has also started.

9:00 A.M.

Early morning

Rush hour

The workday begins

Midmorning

Lunchtime

A rainy afternoon

Evening

Nighttime

Can you find . . .

an artist?

some balloons?

road repair?

At midmorning, the city streets are still busy. People buy food and clothes at the market. New suits arrive at the clothing shop. The museum has opened to visitors. One boy is sure he saw the caveman move. The road workers have broken open a water pipe. Water sprays everywhere! The burglar, meanwhile, gets ready to go to bed.

11:00 A.M.

Early morning

Rush hour

The workday begins

Midmorning

Lunchtime

A rainy afternoon

Evening

Nighttime

Can you find . . .

a museum guide?

a motorcycle rider?

a garbage can?

some actors?

Time for lunch! The students are allowed to leave school. Most of the office workers take a break. Customers fill the cafe. But the weather is taking a turn for the worse. The sky is darkening. The first raindrops fall. A few people take out their umbrellas. Suddenly, a thief grabs somebody's bag in the market. People chase the thief. Meanwhile, the burglar is fast asleep.

1:00 P.M.

Early morning

Rush hour

The workday begins

Midmorning

Lunchtime

A rainy afternoon

Evening

Nighttime

Can you find . . .

a spider?

a TV cameraman?

a man falling?

an umbrella?

some dancers?

Later in the afternoon, the rain is pouring down. Most people huddle under umbrellas. But one couple decides to dance! School has finished for the day. The office workers have a small party. In the museum, a television reporter interviews the boy who saw the caveman move. While the burglar sleeps, another burglar sneaks into his apartment!

4:00 P.M.

Early morning

Rush hour

The workday begins

Midmorning

Lunchtime

A rainy afternoon

Evening

Nighttime

Can you
find . . .

a cat?

a skateboarder?

an art class?

a streetlight?

some theatergoers?

It is early evening. The rain has stopped.
People arrive at the theater. They find
their seats and wait for the performance
to start. An art class takes place in the
school. Some children skateboard in the
empty marketplace. Everyone has left the
museum. The exhibits can move freely! The
burglar wakes up to discover his bag of
stolen goods is gone.

7:30 P.M.

Early morning

Rush hour

The workday begins

Midmorning

Lunchtime

A rainy afternoon

Evening

Nighttime

Can you find . . .

a bat?

a bicyclist?

a sculpture?

a taxi?

a man
walking his dog?

It is late. The play is over. People are on their way home. Only people walking their dogs and a few dancing men are still on the streets. The office worker falls asleep at his desk. The sculptors in the apartment above celebrate. Their whale is finished! One of the museum workers finally sees the moving caveman. Some people leaving the theater catch the burglar. Another busy day in the city has ended!

11:00 P.M.

Early morning

Rush hour

The workday begins

Midmorning

Lunchtime

A rainy afternoon

Evening

Nighttime

Glossary

burglar: a person who breaks into buildings or homes and steals things

caveman: a human who lived in a cave long, long ago

rehearsal: a practice for a performance

sculptors: people who make sculptures

sculpture: something carved or shaped from clay, stone, metal, wood, or another material

sleepwalker: a person who gets out of bed and walks while sleeping

taxi: a car with a driver whom people pay to drive them where they want to go

theatergoers: people who go to the theater to see a play or other performance

Learn More about Cities

Books

Gordon, Sharon. *At Home in the City.* Tarrytown, NY: Marshall Cavendish Benchmark, 2006.

Johnson, Stephen T. *Alphabet City.* New York: Viking, 1995.

Raschka, Chris. *New York Is English, Chattanooga Is Creek.* New York: Atheneum Books for Young Readers, 2005.

Rotner, Shelley. *Senses in the City.* Minneapolis: Millbrook Press, 2008.

Sterling, Kristin. *Living in Urban Communities.* Minneapolis: Lerner Publications Company, 2008.

Websites

City Creator
http://www.citycreator.com/
This site allows you to build your very own city. You choose the roads, buildings, cars, and people for the city.

Local Legacies: Celebrating Community Roots
http://www.loc.gov/folklife/roots/ac-home.html
Check this site to look for events taking place in a city near you.

A Closer Look

This book has a lot to find. Did you see people who showed up again and again? Think about what these people did and saw during the year. If these people kept journals, what would they write? A journal is a book with blank pages where people write down their thoughts. Have you ever kept a journal? What did you write about?

Try making a journal for one of the characters in this book. You will need a pencil and a piece of paper. Choose your character. Give your character a name. Write the name of the time at the top of the page. Underneath, write about the character's life during that time. Pretend you are the character. What do you do all day long? Is your life hard or easy? Why? What have you noticed about the other people in the city? Have you seen anything surprising? What?

Don't worry if you don't know how to spell every word. You can ask a parent or teacher for help if you need to. And be creative!

Index